The Island of Peace

The Kingdom Beyond the Waves

Jessica hintz

United States
2024

Imprint

Book Title: The Island of Peace - The Kingdom Beyond the Waves
Author: Jessica Hintz

© 2024, Jessica Hintz
All rights reserved.

Author: Jessica Hintz
Contact: boxingboy898337@gmail.com

CONTENTS

Chapter 1: The Mystical Encounter by the Shore

Chapter 2: The Arrival of the Majestic Steed

Chapter 3: The Ride of Fate

Chapter 4: A Rush to the Rock Castle

Chapter 5: The Witch of the Dark Woods

Chapter 6: Lost in the Wilds

Chapter 7: The Stranger's Aid

Chapter 8: The Unseen Bonds of Love

Chapter 9: A Place of Comfort

Chapter 10: A Glimmer of Hope

Chapter 11: The Enchanting Melody

Chapter 12: A Joyful Reunion

Chapter 13: A Friend's Warning

Chapter 14: A Celebration at Sea Castle

Chapter 15: Journey into the Unknown

Chapter 16: Schemes in the Shadows

Chapter 17: Enchanted Discoveries

Chapter 18: The Legend of the Peaceful Kingdom

Chapter 19: A Joyful Reunion and a Royal Wedding

Chapter 20: A Wedding to Unite Two Worlds

Chapter 21 A Royal Ascension

Chapter 22: The Farewell Voyage

Chapter 23: A Royal Encounter

Chapter 24: The Queen's Visit and the Peace Treaty

Chapter 25: A Realm of Lasting Harmony

Chapter 1: The Mystical Encounter by the Shore

Rosemary Evans wandered along the shore, the golden hues of the setting sun casting a warm glow across the endless horizon of shimmering waves. As she walked, her eyes remained fixed on the grand Sea Castle that stood proudly in the distance, its elegant towers rising against the sky. It was her father's domain, a majestic estate overlooking the vast, restless ocean. Yet despite the beauty of the scene and the riches she was born into, a feeling of unease lingered in her heart.

She was the only daughter of Sir Gerald Evans, a man whose name was synonymous with wealth and influence in England. Yet, in spite of her privileged life, Rosemary found little joy in her father's recent remarriage to the widow of the Earl of Pearlsbury. The union, though celebrated by society, had left Rosemary with a gnawing sense of loneliness.

Her mother, Lady Evans, had died when Rosemary was just ten years old. Since that tragic loss, her father had been her only source of comfort and companionship. The memories of her mother still haunted her, and now, the presence of another woman in her father's life only deepened her sense of abandonment. For the first time in years, she felt as if she was adrift, her heart yearning for the love and attention that had once been so abundant.

Tears welled up in Rosemary's eyes as she walked along the beach, her thoughts clouded by the loneliness she had begun to feel more acutely with each passing day.

She whispered a silent prayer to God, asking for peace, for solace, for something to ease the ache in her heart.

As she continued her walk, her gaze was drawn to something unusual near the water's edge. She stopped and squinted into the fading light, trying to make sense of the strange sight before her. There, lying on the damp sand, was a small, exhausted seahorse, its delicate body barely moving. Beside it, almost as if it had been placed there intentionally, was a small, ornate box.

Curiosity piqued, Rosemary bent down and carefully lifted the box. The moment her fingers touched its smooth surface, a strange warmth seemed to radiate from it, and before she could fully comprehend what was happening, the seahorse began to glow. It shone brightly, almost blinding her. The light was so intense that she had to shut her eyes, unable to bear the brightness.

When she opened them again, she could hardly believe what she saw. In place of the seahorse stood a magnificent white horse, its coat gleaming like snow in the fading light. The creature was tall, elegant, and exuded a sense of grace and strength. Rosemary froze for a moment, her heart racing in her chest. A wave of fear swept over her, though she couldn't quite explain why. The horse was beautiful, but its sudden appearance, coupled with the strange glow, left her feeling uneasy.

"Did I imagine it?" she thought, trying to rationalize the moment. "Perhaps it arrived just now, in the blink of an eye."

Taking a deep breath, Rosemary shook off her momentary panic and glanced around. The shore was empty, with no sign of anyone nearby who might have claimed the horse. It seemed, impossibly, to belong to no one but her. Tentatively, she reached out and placed her hand on the soft, velvety neck of the animal. The horse nickered softly in response, as if it recognized her touch and welcomed it.

A sense of peace washed over her, and the anxiety that had gripped her moments ago began to fade. She couldn't bring herself to leave the horse behind. It was too beautiful, too gentle, and she felt an inexplicable bond with it, as though it had been waiting for her all along. With a final glance at the mysterious box, which she still held in her hand, she decided to take the horse with her.

As she walked back towards the Sea Castle, the white horse followed her silently, its hoofbeats soft against the sand. Rosemary looked over her shoulder and was surprised to see that it was still there, trailing behind her as if it had been hers all along. She had no idea where it had come from or why it had appeared, but she felt a strange sense of purpose as she led it up the path towards the castle gates.

The horse, though large and imposing, seemed to carry no hint of threat. Instead, it moved with a calm grace, its presence reassuring in a way that Rosemary couldn't quite explain. She smiled as she touched the animal's neck again, feeling a connection that transcended logic or reason. It was as though she had found a companion, a friend, in this magnificent creature.

The evening air was cool as Rosemary approached the castle, but the warmth of the horse's presence kept her comforted. It was a strange and magical moment, one that seemed to blur the line between reality and something more fantastical. But in that moment, Rosemary didn't question it. She simply accepted it, allowing herself to be enveloped by the magic of the encounter.

As she entered the castle, the horse followed her without hesitation, its hooves echoing on the stone floor. Rosemary's heart swelled with a mixture of wonder and gratitude. She had come to the shore seeking solace, and somehow, in the most unexpected of ways, she had found it. She wasn't sure what the future held, or why the horse had appeared, but she knew that for the first time in a long while, she didn't feel so alone.

The horse stood silently beside her, its head turned toward her as though it were waiting for her next move. She placed the box carefully on a nearby table and stroked the horse's mane. The soft, silky strands slipped through her fingers like a gentle breeze. It was then that she realized the horse wasn't just a beautiful creature—it was something more. A symbol of something greater, something she couldn't yet understand.

The magical glow of the seahorse, the appearance of the horse, the box—it all felt like a dream, or perhaps a sign. But whatever it was, Rosemary knew that her life had changed in that fleeting moment by the shore. The sadness and loneliness that had once consumed her seemed to have faded into the background, replaced by a new sense of wonder and possibility.

As the evening drew to a close and the last of the sunlight disappeared beyond the horizon, Rosemary couldn't help but feel a spark of hope flicker in her heart. The horse, now a part of her world, would remain by her side, offering her strength and companionship in the days to come. She wasn't sure where the journey would lead, but for the first time in a long while, she was ready to embrace whatever came next.

And as the castle loomed before her, its turrets darkening in the twilight, Rosemary Evans knew that her life, though complicated and uncertain, had taken an extraordinary turn. The shore had given her a gift—one that would carry her into a future filled with both mystery and magic.

Chapter 2: The Arrival of the Majestic Steed

The gates of Sea Castle opened wide as Rosemary Evans arrived with the magnificent white horse at her side. The guards, who had long been accustomed to the comings and goings of the estate, were taken aback by the sight of the elegant creature that followed her. It was a stunning spectacle—one they had never witnessed before—and their faces lit up with delight as they saw Rosemary approach.

"Miss Rosemary!" one of the guards called out as he gave a respectful nod. "What a marvelous horse you have brought with you today."

Rosemary offered a graceful smile and returned their salute. "I found this horse by the seashore," she explained. "There was no one around, so I decided to bring it here. It seems to be tame and quite intelligent. I trust you will treat it kindly and look after it."

"At your service, Miss!" the guards replied in unison, bowing deeply before her. Their admiration for both the horse and Rosemary was clear. They stood aside as she walked past them, moving with quiet elegance towards the castle doors, the horse trailing closely behind her.

Once inside, Rosemary gave instructions to the stablemen to treat the horse with the utmost care. "I want it groomed thoroughly," she said, "and fitted with the finest saddle, stirrups, and matching accessories in a brilliant white. I want it ready to ride in a week's time." She spoke with an air of quiet authority, and the men nodded in agreement, eager to follow her commands.

With the horse's care taken care of, Rosemary retreated to her room to secure the mysterious box she had found alongside the creature. She placed it carefully among her other precious jewels, locking it in a small chest with the key safely hidden away. Rosemary didn't dare to open the box—not yet, anyway. The strange glow of the seahorse and the sudden appearance of the white horse left her with suspicions that she couldn't ignore. What did the box hold? Was there something more to the horse than she knew?

She didn't know, but she wasn't ready to uncover its secrets just yet.

Meanwhile, the horse was treated like royalty by the stablehands. Rosemary's instructions were clear, and they spared no effort in pampering the magnificent creature. It was fed the best food from the castle's stores, and its coat was polished to perfection. The white horse quickly became the envy of the other horses in the stable, standing out with its immaculate beauty and grace. It was impossible not to notice the aura of elegance it carried—an aura that seemed to elevate the very air around it.

That evening, the castle was alive with a sense of excitement. A new guest, a royal guest, had arrived, and it was no surprise that the presence of the horse was the talk of the estate. Sir Gerald Evans, Rosemary's father, and his new bride, Lady Evans, were among the first to admire the creature.

"What a magnificent animal, my dear," Sir Gerald said, his eyes wide with admiration as he observed the horse. "I must say, I've never seen anything quite like it."

Lady Evans, smiling warmly, added, "It's a beauty. Thank you, Rosemary, for bringing it into our lives. It will be a splendid addition to the castle."

Rosemary felt a brief moment of pride, but it was quickly overshadowed by the presence of Lady Evans. Despite the praise, there was something unsettling about her new stepmother's words, and the constant reminder of the changes in her life made it difficult to enjoy the moment fully.

Later, as the family gathered in the castle's grand hall, the conversation turned to the horse once again. Lady Evans, her eyes sparkling with excitement, expressed her wish to ride the animal with Sir Gerald. "Wouldn't it be wonderful, Gerald?" she said. "Such a majestic creature should be ridden, don't you think?"

Rosemary felt a flicker of unease in her chest. The horse had been so calm with her, but the idea of others riding it seemed to unsettle her. There was something about it that felt so unique, so fragile, that she couldn't shake the feeling that it should be kept safe. Still, she didn't want to seem overly protective, so she hesitated before responding.

"It does seem friendly enough," Rosemary said, trying to mask her concern. "But perhaps we should give it some time to settle in. It's still new to the castle."

Laura, the governess, who had been standing quietly in the background, suddenly spoke up. "I'm not so sure about this idea," she said, her voice firm and skeptical. "That horse might be wild, despite its calm demeanor. It's always better to be cautious with such animals."

Rosemary turned to face her. "But it seems so gentle," she countered, trying to reassure Laura. "I've had no trouble with it at all."

Laura raised an eyebrow. "I've seen enough horses in my time to know that appearances can be deceiving. You may want to rethink this."

"I think we can trust it," Rosemary said, her tone more confident now. "I'm certain it will be fine. Father, don't you agree?"

Sir Gerald, who had been listening quietly, finally spoke. "I think Rosemary is right," he said, his voice calm but authoritative. "We shall give it a chance. If it proves to be well-behaved, then it's no harm to let Lady Evans have a ride."

Rosemary smiled in relief, glad that her father had sided with her. She glanced at Laura, who appeared less than pleased, but there was nothing she could do. The decision had been made.

Lady Evans, thrilled by the approval, clapped her hands together. "Wonderful! We shall make plans to ride it tomorrow. I can't wait to take a turn on such a splendid horse."

Rosemary could see that her stepmother was already envisioning herself atop the horse, but part of her remained uneasy. She couldn't shake the feeling that the horse was hers, that it belonged to her alone. Still, she kept her thoughts to herself and tried to enjoy the evening.

For the rest of the night, the castle was filled with chatter and laughter. The horse had become the center of attention, admired by all who had seen it. Rosemary couldn't help but feel a strange mix of pride and protectiveness, but she also couldn't deny that the beauty of the creature had brought a sense of joy to the castle that had been missing for some time. Sir Gerald seemed pleased, Lady Evans was delighted, and the guests who had gathered for the evening admired the horse's elegance and grace.

Yet amidst all the excitement, there was one person who remained silent and somewhat distant—Laura, the governess. Her disapproval was clear, but it was of no consequence. The playful spirit of the Evans family had taken over, and the evening was filled with laughter and the promise of new adventures. For everyone, except the governess, it was a wonderful evening at the Sea Castle.

As the night wore on, Rosemary retreated to her room, her mind racing with thoughts of the white horse. She had no idea what would happen next, but she knew one thing for certain: her life had changed the moment she found it on the shore, and she wasn't sure where this strange journey would take her.

Chapter 3: The Ride of Fate

After a week of meticulous care and training, the day had finally arrived. The horse, which had been carefully monitored and prepared for the journey, was ready for its first ride. Rosemary awoke before the crack of dawn, her anticipation palpable as she made preparations for the day ahead. Her maids helped her into her traveling attire—light, comfortable clothing suited for a ride, with a cloak draped over her shoulders to protect her from the morning chill. She issued a few final instructions, ensuring everything was in order for the ride ahead, before making her way outside.

Her governess, Laura, was already preparing to ride as well. The governess had been Rosemary's constant companion since she was a young girl, riding alongside her on every excursion since Rosemary's very first pony ride at the tender age of thirteen. She was a stern woman, ever watchful of Rosemary's safety, particularly when it came to riding. Even now, after all these years, Laura was as cautious as ever, determined not to let Rosemary ride too quickly for fear of injury.

Accompanied by ten of their armed men, whose sole purpose was to protect the ladies, they set off on their journey. The men were well-trained, capable of defending the ladies if necessary, but they knew their primary duty was to ensure the safety of Rosemary and her governess. The trail they followed was winding and serene, flanked by towering trees on either side, their branches casting soft shadows across the ground.

As they began their ride, Rosemary could not help but notice the serene beauty of the early morning. The mist, still lingering in the air, slowly dissipated with the warmth of the sun's rays. The flowers along the trail seemed to awaken as well, their colors more vivid, and their scents more fragrant, as if they, too, were greeting Rosemary. Tiny drops of dew clung to the leaves of the trees, glistening in the sunlight, making the scene appear magical, almost otherworldly. It felt as though nature itself was blessing her, and for a brief moment, she felt at peace with the world.

Riding the horse felt unlike anything Rosemary had experienced before. The ride was smooth, almost effortless, and the animal seemed to glide across the terrain with a grace that was both enchanting and surreal. For the first time in her life, Rosemary felt a deep connection with the creature beneath her. It was as if the horse was an extension of herself, moving in perfect harmony with her every thought and desire.

She glanced back over her shoulder to see the governess and the men trailing behind. Laura, as expected, was not able to keep up with Rosemary's pace. The governess was calling out to her, urging her to slow down. "Rosemary, please!" Laura's voice carried across the air, tinged with concern. "You must slow down! It could be dangerous!" Her words were laced with the same caution that had marked every ride since Rosemary was a child.

But Rosemary, caught up in the exhilaration of the moment, barely heard her. "It must be a wild horse," Laura muttered under her breath, her worry growing with every passing moment.

Rosemary, however, felt no fear. She didn't understand why, but she knew, deep down, that the horse would not harm her. It was as though she and the horse shared some unspoken bond, a trust forged in the quiet moments they had spent together. But as the distance between them grew, and the governess's cries became more distant, Rosemary's heart fluttered with a sense of unease. Could it be that the horse was truly wild? Or was it something more—something that connected her to forces beyond her understanding?

The ride continued, and Rosemary was soon several yards ahead of the governess and the men. The world around her seemed to blur as the horse moved faster, its hooves pounding the earth with a rhythmic precision. The further they went, the more Rosemary felt an inexplicable pull, as though something was guiding them forward, pushing them toward an unknown destination.

Suddenly, the horse's pace quickened, its speed becoming almost supernatural. Before Rosemary could react, the creature veered off the path, galloping at a pace so swift it was like the wind itself had taken hold of them. Rosemary gripped the reins tighter, but the horse seemed to be in complete control, taking them further into the woods at an alarming speed. To her surprise, though, she didn't feel the usual panic that would accompany such a fast ride. In fact, she didn't feel tired or out of breath at all. The horse seemed to move without effort, as if guided by an unseen force.

After what seemed like an eternity, the horse finally came to a halt beneath the canopy of a large oak tree deep in the woods. Rosemary, though shaken, was not frightened. She dismounted slowly, her thoughts a whirlwind of confusion. What had just happened? The woods around her felt oddly silent, the air heavy with an unspoken presence. She stood there for a moment, trying to make sense of what had transpired.

Suddenly, a brilliant flash of light appeared before her, and a soft, melodious voice filled the air. The voice called her name—clear, sweet, and musical, as though it was floating on the breeze.

"Rosemary... Rosemary..." the voice sang, echoing through the trees.

Startled, Rosemary looked around, trying to locate the source of the voice. "Who is this?" she called out, her heart racing. "What's going on? What do you want from me?"

The voice replied, soothing and calm. "The Seahorse is yours, Rosemary. You are its rightful owner, for as long as you are destined to be glorified on the Island of Peace. Do not fear. Keep it with you, for it shall leave when your mission is complete."

Rosemary stood motionless, struggling to process the words. "What mission?" she asked, her voice trembling with uncertainty.

"The pearl box you took from the horse is a symbol of a promise," the voice explained. "A promise that will bring glory and wealth to the people of the Island of Peace. But beware. The Witch of the Dark Woods seeks to steal it from you, and she has enlisted the help of Sir Grey Winkle, who is invited to the ball this evening. You must take the box and secure it in your father's Rock Castle, amidst the evergreen woods where you once lived with your mother."

The voice paused, then added, "You must do this alone. Do not step off the path until you reach the castle. If you do, you will be lost forever. The pearl box will protect you, but only if you trust it. Do not entrust it to anyone else."

The voice was fading now, its final words lingering in the air like a blessing. "Help will come to you, Rosemary. And in time, you will find your true love. May success be yours. God be with you."

With that, the light vanished, and the voice fell silent. Rosemary stood in the quiet woods, her heart pounding in her chest. She looked around, still processing the incredible encounter.

Suddenly, a sense of urgency washed over her. She needed to return to the Sea Castle before it was too late.

She turned and hurried back along the path, her thoughts racing. The moment she reappeared on the trail, she saw her governess and the men searching desperately for her. Their relief was palpable when they spotted her, and they quickly fell into line behind her as she made her way back to the Sea Castle. The governess, though visibly shaken, was overjoyed to see Rosemary unharmed.

As they made their way back to the castle, Rosemary couldn't help but wonder: what had just happened? What was the mission she had been chosen for? And most importantly—who was the voice that had spoken to her in the woods?

One thing was certain: her life had changed forever. And a new journey had only just begun.

Chapter 4: A Rush to the Rock Castle

As the dinner bell rang through the halls of the Sea Castle, Rosemary entered quietly, but her thoughts were far from the evening meal. With a sense of urgency, she bypassed the great dining room and made her way directly to her private chamber. The air was heavy with the weight of her decision, and every step she took felt like a step toward an uncertain fate.

Once in her room, Rosemary wasted no time. She walked straight to the chest that sat at the foot of her bed, the one where she had concealed the Pearl Box. With delicate hands, she opened the chest and retrieved the box. She cradled it gently, as though it were the most precious thing in the world. Its cool surface felt reassuring against her skin, but the weight of its significance was far more pressing. After a few moments of hesitation, she slipped the box into the deep pocket of her cloak, making sure it was secure.

Her mind raced as she stood by the door, her eyes flickering to the corridor beyond. Her heart pounded, a mixture of fear and resolve settling in her chest. She had been given a task—an important mission—and now, there was no turning back.

But before stepping out, Rosemary stopped. She turned back towards the room, towards the beautiful cross that hung on the wall. Dropping to her knees, she closed her eyes and prayed. The words tumbled from her lips with an urgency that matched the tension in her heart.

"Please, God," she whispered, her voice trembling slightly. "If this is not Your will, stop me. But if it is, grant me the strength to see it through. Protect me, and protect the people of the Island of Peace." Her words were simple, but they carried the weight of the world. She prayed for guidance, for clarity, and for the courage to face whatever lay ahead.

When she finished, she stood, her resolve solidified. She took a deep breath, wiped away the lingering doubts, and walked towards the door.

As she stepped into the hallway, her governess appeared from around the corner. She had been anxiously waiting, and her face immediately showed concern.

"Is everything all right, my lady?" the governess asked, eyeing Rosemary closely.

Rosemary forced a smile, masking the uncertainty that churned inside her. "Yes, everything is fine. I just need to attend to something important, but I'll return soon. I promise."

The governess raised an eyebrow but said nothing more. Rosemary knew she had to keep up the façade, to move forward as though nothing had changed.

Before she could move past the governess, her father's voice called out to her from the other end of the hall. "Rosemary, where are you going so late in the evening?" His tone was warm, but his eyes held a glint of concern.

Without missing a beat, Rosemary turned toward him. "I'm heading to the Rock Castle, Father. There's something I must attend to."

Gerald's brow furrowed in confusion. "But you haven't eaten since dawn, my dear. You must be starving after such a long ride."

"I'll be fine, Father," Rosemary said in her sweet, melodic voice. "I will return for the ball later. Don't worry about me." She smiled affectionately, a smile that held the same warmth and charm it always had. Then, with a graceful bow, she turned on her heel and walked briskly toward the door.

Her father watched her for a moment, his concern still palpable, but he didn't question her further. Trusting his daughter implicitly, he allowed her to go.

As Rosemary made her way down the hall and out of the castle, her father's men attempted to follow her, worried about her solitary journey. However, she stopped them, her voice firm but gentle. "No need to accompany me. I must do this alone."

They hesitated but ultimately respected her wishes, though they continued to watch from a distance. They were no match for her speed, and soon she was out of sight, riding faster than they could manage.

Back inside the castle, Gerald stood at the window, staring out into the night. His mind was troubled, a knot of unease forming in his chest. He had sent men to follow Rosemary, but they had returned without her. They were unable to keep up with her on horseback, and that troubled him deeply.

In his heart, Gerald knew something was different about this journey. Rosemary was not just going to the Rock

Castle as she had claimed. She was running towards something—something unknown, yet undeniably urgent.

With a heavy heart, he sent his men ahead to the Rock Castle to wait for her return. There was little he could do except wait and pray for her safe return.

Chapter 5: The Witch of the Dark Woods

Meanwhile, deep within the Dark Woods, the Witch of the Woods stood hunched over her crystal ball, her eyes fixed on the image that appeared before her. She cackled, her voice echoing through the trees like a distant storm.

"Ah, my rival," she said, her voice dripping with malice as she observed Rosemary riding swiftly through the night. The Pearl Box, glowing softly in Rosemary's cloak, caught her attention, and the witch's grin widened.

"My prey," she hissed, her voice laced with sarcasm. "You think you can thwart me? I shall make you run madly between your castles, while Sir Winkle searches for you in vain."

She laughed cruelly, her voice a thunderous roar that shook the very ground beneath her. "Once the box is mine, I will rule the Island of Peace! Its people will be my slaves, and its beasts, my feast. This island, with its spellbound riches, shall be mine!"

The witch's laughter filled the air, drowning out the sounds of the forest, as if the woods themselves trembled at her wicked intentions.

Her eyes glinted with rage as she watched Rosemary riding alone, unaware of the dangers closing in on her. "You are but a worm beneath my feet," the witch sneered, "soon to be crushed beneath the weight of my power."

She leaned closer to the crystal ball, her fingers curling with anticipation. Everything was falling into place. The Pearl Box would soon be hers, and with it, the key to her domination over the Island of Peace.

As Rosemary sped toward her destiny, the witch's eyes burned with fury. Her plans would not fail. Not this time.

Chapter 6: Lost in the Wilds

Rosemary galloped through the forest towards the Rock Castle, just a few miles away from the sea. The path she followed was familiar to her—an old, winding road that cut through the heart of the woods and led to the Castle. As she rode, she couldn't help but admire the untouched beauty of the forest, its towering trees and thick foliage swaying in the cool breeze. It was a sight she had seen countless times, but today it seemed more vivid, more alive. The sense of freedom it gave her was far more exhilarating than the view from her coach, which felt like a mere cage by comparison.

But in the midst of her reverie, she forgot the instructions she had received. A flash of movement caught her eye—a sleek, white hare bounding gracefully across the path. Without a second thought, she spurred the horse to a stop, her mind consumed with the idea of chasing after it. To her, the hunt was a way to taste the sweetness of freedom, the joy of being unrestrained, with no royal obligations to weigh her down.

She urged the horse forward, leaping from its back to run after the hare, her heart pounding with excitement. She had always thought of herself as a free spirit, someone untouched by the constraints of her noble birth. But little did she know, this impulsive decision would soon lead her into danger, a trap set by forces far darker than she could have imagined.

The chase lasted only a few moments before the hare darted into a thicket, disappearing from her sight. Rosemary stopped in her tracks, out of breath and momentarily disoriented. She glanced around, trying to regain her bearings. The road she had been following had now become difficult to trace, obscured by the dense undergrowth and twisting vines. It was strange—she had never taken this long to reach the Castle before. The woods, once familiar, now felt vast and foreboding.

Her heart sank as she realized that she had lost her way. She was now deep within the woods, far from both the Rock Castle and the Sea Castle. Sunset was approaching, and she knew there was no way she could make it to either place before dark. Despair began to claw at her as she stood helplessly, unsure of which direction to take. Her chest tightened with anxiety as she began to weep, praying desperately for guidance, for some sign to show her the way.

Just as she had given up hope, a low, rumbling sound reached her ears. It was the sound of hounds—hunting dogs, and they were coming closer with every passing second. Her heart leapt into her throat, and panic surged through her veins. The hounds were only a few yards away now, their snarls and growls growing louder. She could hear the snap of their jaws, hungry and vicious. Rosemary screamed for help, her voice trembling with terror.

Chapter 7: The Stranger's Aid

The hounds were almost upon her when she closed her eyes, bracing herself for the inevitable. But just as she felt the first brush of fear, she heard something that made her open her eyes in disbelief. A voice—strong, calm, and commanding—spoke out from the darkness.

"Stay back!" the voice ordered.

And there, standing tall between Rosemary and the approaching hounds, was a young man, his sword raised high. He was a warrior, and with each powerful swing of his blade, he struck fear into the pack of dogs. The hounds, though fierce, cowered before his might. They tried to lunge, but he met each one with swift, precise movements.

"Get back, beasts!" he shouted, and with a final swipe of his sword, the pack of hounds fled, retreating into the woods.

Rosemary, wide-eyed and trembling, watched in awe as the young man dispatched the hounds with remarkable skill. The tension in her body slowly began to ease as she realized she was no longer in immediate danger. She breathed a sigh of relief and took a step forward, her voice filled with gratitude.

"Thank you," she said softly, her voice cracking. "I don't know what would have happened if you hadn't come."

The young man turned to her, his face kind but with an air of quiet strength. He gave her a gentle smile, one that seemed to put her at ease despite the situation.

"It's nothing," he replied modestly. "I heard your cry, and I could not stand by. You're safe now."

Rosemary felt a strange sense of admiration for him. He was unlike any man she had ever seen. Tall and broad-shouldered, he had the look of someone who had been trained in the arts of battle. But there was a softness to his eyes, a kindness that belied his warrior's exterior. He was, in a word, handsome—far more so than any nobleman she had ever encountered.

"I'm Ferdinand," he introduced himself, his voice warm and sincere. "I came after my lamb, and when I heard you calling for help, I couldn't let you face those hounds alone."

Rosemary, still in a daze from the encounter, blinked in surprise. "Ferdinand? I'm Rosemary," she said, her voice steadying. "I... I ran after a hare and lost my way. And then the hounds... they came for me. I never thought anyone would come to help."

Ferdinand's eyes softened with sympathy as he looked at her. "I'm glad I arrived when I did," he said. "It seems God sent me here for a reason."

Rosemary nodded, her heart swelling with gratitude. "It must have been divine intervention," she whispered.

Ferdinand smiled again, his gaze lingering on her for a moment longer than necessary. "No one should be alone in the woods at night," he said. "Let me help you find your way back."

The two of them set off together, walking in the direction of the village. The journey was quiet, with only the sound of their footsteps and the occasional rustling of the trees. Rosemary felt a strange sense of comfort in his presence. There was something about him—something reassuring—that made her feel safe despite the circumstances. She found herself glancing at him more than once, admiring his strong yet gentle demeanor.

As they walked, they passed by a small pond, its waters shimmering under the fading light of day. The surface was dotted with vibrant water lilies, their petals a brilliant shade of pink. Rosemary stopped in her tracks, captivated by the sight.

"Look," she said, pointing towards the lilies. "They're so beautiful."

Ferdinand looked over at the pond and then back at her. "Do you want some?" he asked, raising an eyebrow.

Rosemary nodded eagerly. "I would love some."

But as she moved towards the water, it became clear that she would have to wade into the shallows to reach the lilies. Ferdinand, ever the gentleman, quickly set down his lamb and moved to stop her.

"Nay, young lady," he said with a laugh. "I will get them for you."

Rosemary smiled, touched by his kindness. "You're too kind, Ferdinand," she said softly. "But I can fetch them myself."

"No," he insisted, his voice playful. "I insist. You should not have to get your feet wet."

With that, Ferdinand waded into the pond, carefully gathering the lilies for her. Rosemary watched him, her heart fluttering. She had never met anyone like him before, and for a moment, it felt as if they had known each other for years.

When he returned with the lilies, Rosemary took them from his hands, her fingers brushing against his for a brief moment. Their eyes met, and for an instant, the world around them seemed to disappear.

"Thank you," she said, her voice soft but filled with warmth. "You've been so kind. I don't know how to repay you."

Ferdinand smiled, his eyes filled with a quiet confidence. "There's no need to repay me," he said simply. "I'm just glad I could help."

Together, they continued their walk through the woods, the bond between them growing with each step. Neither of them could have known, but this was the beginning of something much larger—something that would change their lives forever.

Chapter 8: The Unseen Bonds of Love

Rosemary's foot slipped as she stepped too close to the edge of the pond, and in an instant, she was swept away, her body plunging into the cool water. The shock of it was immediate, and she gasped in horror as she struggled to stay afloat. Ferdinand, who had been walking behind, lunged forward with impressive speed and grasped her hands just in time. He hauled her out of the water, pulling her back to solid ground in a swift motion. Only her head and hands had been visible above the surface, but it was enough to make his heart race with concern.

"I would have gotten them for you," Ferdinand said, his voice a mixture of relief and exasperation. "But you wouldn't listen."

Rosemary, her heart still pounding from the near-drowning experience, realized just how much Ferdinand cared for her. She had seen the panic in his eyes as he reached for her, and it filled her with an overwhelming sense of gratitude. She thanked him again for saving her life, her voice trembling slightly as she spoke.

But then, something strange happened. Ferdinand paused, a look of disbelief crossing his face as he gazed around them. "I don't believe my eyes…" he murmured, his voice tinged with awe and confusion.

Rosemary followed his gaze, and her own heart skipped a beat. The pond, which had just moments ago been a tranquil body of water, had vanished. In its place, there was nothing but rolling pastures and shrubs, as if the pond had never existed at all.

"What is this?" Ferdinand whispered, his brow furrowing in confusion.

Rosemary, too, was stunned. She had no explanation, but the unease that settled in her chest was palpable. She didn't know who or what could be responsible for such a strange phenomenon, but it seemed clear that they were caught in something far beyond their understanding.

"I trust you," Ferdinand said, his gaze locking with hers. "But this... this is unearthly. Who would seek to harm someone as kind and innocent as you?"

Rosemary, feeling both comforted and unsettled by his words, took a deep breath and began to tell him her story. She explained who she was and what had led her to this strange encounter in the woods. Ferdinand listened intently, his expression a mix of disbelief and concern. When she finished, he shook his head in astonishment.

"Sir Gerald Evans," he said thoughtfully, "is known for his kindness and honor. It is an honor to be of help to his daughter. And if you'll allow me, I will continue to protect you. I'll stand by your side through this mission of yours."

Rosemary was touched by his words, and she could scarcely believe that a complete stranger would offer such loyalty and protection. It felt like a dream, one that was almost too wonderful to be true.

"It is my pleasure," she replied, her voice soft and dreamy, as if she were floating on air.

Ferdinand smiled, clearly pleased by her response. And for the first time in a long while, Rosemary allowed herself to feel truly happy. It seemed as if the bonds of fate had already begun to weave their story together, one they were both powerless to resist.

They moved swiftly through the woods, eager to leave behind the mystery and danger that seemed to lurk at every turn. Ferdinand, ever the protector, fashioned a beautiful garland of wildflowers and a crown made from the most stunning blossoms of the valley. He placed the garland in Rosemary's hair, and she accepted the gift with a smile that seemed to light up the entire forest.

They continued on their journey, and soon they came across a group of shepherds leading their flocks toward the village. The shepherds, seeing Ferdinand with the beautiful young lady, immediately began to sing songs in praise of their love. The melodies were simple but filled with joy, and the songs seemed to uplift the spirits of both Ferdinand and Rosemary. The couple walked hand in hand, their hearts light with the hope of a future neither had anticipated but both now longed for.

As they entered the village, the atmosphere was one of warmth and community. The villagers greeted Ferdinand and Rosemary with smiles, and there was a sense of celebration in the air, as if the union of these two hearts had been awaited for years. The shepherds' songs echoed through the village, adding to the enchantment of the moment.

When they reached the farmhouse, they were greeted by two young children—Ferdinand's niece and nephew, Edward and Annie. The children, full of energy and excitement, ran up to Ferdinand, eager to see their beloved uncle. Rosemary, still dazed by the events of the day, watched with a gentle smile as the children embraced Ferdinand with open arms.

Ferdinand turned to his brother Oswald and his wife to explain what had transpired. He told them of the danger that had threatened Rosemary, how he had found her in the woods and saved her from the hounds. He spoke of the mysterious disappearance of the pond and the strange forces at work. Oswald and his wife were delighted to meet Rosemary, and they welcomed her into their home with open arms.

"Thank you for everything," Rosemary said, her heart full of gratitude. "I don't know how I would have made it through without you."

Ferdinand, ever humble, waved her thanks aside. "It was nothing," he said, his smile warm. "But I promised your father I would keep you safe. And I intend to do just that."

With a final look of reassurance, Ferdinand bid his family farewell and set off for the Sea Castle, determined to let the Evans know that their daughter was safe and well. The journey was long, but his heart was light, knowing that Rosemary was in good hands with his family.

Meanwhile, back at the Sea Castle, Sir Gerald and Lady Evans were in the depths of despair. The ball, which was meant to be a celebration, had turned into a night of worry and anguish. Sir Gerald could hardly contain his anxiety, his every thought consumed by the disappearance of his daughter. He paced the halls, his mind racing with possibilities of what could have happened to her.

"She must have stayed at the Castle," Lady Evans said, trying to comfort her husband. "She's probably just tired from the long ride."

But deep down, she knew something was terribly wrong. The governess, too, was filled with dread, though she kept her suspicions to herself, fearful of adding to the mounting worry. She had wondered aloud if it had been a wild horse that had thrown Rosemary, but she kept those thoughts hidden, not wanting to distress the family further.

As the night wore on, Sir Gerald became increasingly restless. He had no peace, no comfort, as thoughts of his daughter's safety plagued him. He had sent men to search for her, but they had returned empty-handed. The housekeeper at the Rock Castle denied having seen Rosemary, and the confusion only deepened.

The hours stretched on, each moment feeling longer than the last. Sir Gerald had nightmares, vivid and disturbing dreams of his daughter being in danger—attacked by wild animals, kidnapped by strangers, or worse. He could not shake the feeling of dread that settled in his chest, and sleep eluded him completely.

Lady Evans, too, was on edge. She spent the night praying for Rosemary's safe return, her thoughts consumed with worry for her daughter. The governess joined her in prayer, both of them hoping against hope that their beloved Rosemary would come home soon.

Chapter 9: A Place of Comfort

Rosemary had never experienced a sense of warmth and safety like she did in the humble farmhouse of Ferdinand's family. The atmosphere was simple, yet it felt more like home than the cold, imposing walls of her royal castle ever had. It wasn't just the physical comfort that soothed her, but the kindness and genuine care she received from the people around her. That evening, Rosemary shared a modest yet delicious meal with Ferdinand's family, savoring every bite. It was far removed from the lavish feasts of her life at the castle, but it filled her heart in a way that those royal indulgences never could.

Here, in the modest farmhouse, she felt liberated. There were no rigid rules about how to behave, no expectations of decorum, no need to sit up straight or speak in a carefully measured tone. Instead, she could relax and be herself. There was no need for pretenses or forced elegance. She had the freedom to laugh, eat, and converse like any other woman.

Ferdinand, the young man who had saved her life, was everything she had ever imagined a man of virtue to be. At twenty-four, he had already become a figure of admiration, known for his bravery, charm, and intellect. His appearance was that of a knight in shining armor, not just in his looks but in his heart as well. He was a man of great education, fluent in Latin, Greek, French, and English. He carried himself with grace and humility, which made him beloved by all who knew him.

Ferdinand was also a man marked by hardship. After losing both of his parents, he was raised by his older brother Oswald and his wife, who treated him as one of their own children. The bond between Ferdinand and his adoptive family was one of love and mutual respect. It was evident that he had learned from them the true meaning of kindness and generosity, qualities that made him all the more desirable in Rosemary's eyes.

As she lay in the soft bed that had been specially prepared for her, Rosemary reflected on the simplicity of her life in the farmhouse. "How strange it is," she thought, "to find such happiness in a life so far removed from the one I knew." Her life as a royal lady had been filled with luxury, but it had also been full of constraints. Here, in the warmth of the farmhouse, she could breathe freely. For the first time, she felt like a real person rather than a figurehead.

The room was quiet except for the soft sounds of the night and the occasional crackling of the fire. Rosemary closed her eyes, filled with gratitude for the protection she had received. She thanked God for guiding her to this place, for saving her life and bringing her to a family that had shown her such kindness. Her thoughts turned to Ferdinand. The more she thought about him, the more she realized how much he meant to her. She knew, without a doubt, that she had never felt so alive as she did in his presence.

Her mind wandered, filled with thoughts of love, gratitude, and hope. As she drifted off to sleep, she whispered a prayer for the well-being of the kind family that had opened their hearts and home to her. In her dreams, she saw Ferdinand's face, his gentle eyes and kind smile, and she felt an overwhelming sense of peace wash over her.

Chapter 10: A Glimmer of Hope

The moon was high in the sky when Ferdinand finally arrived at the Sea Castle, bringing with him the long-awaited news of Rosemary's safety. It was a little past eleven when he stepped into the grand hall, and the atmosphere in the castle was heavy with anxiety. Sir Gerald and Lady Evans had been on edge all night, their worry growing with each passing hour. But the moment they heard that their daughter was safe, their faces lit up with relief.

Ferdinand explained how Rosemary had been rescued from the pack of hounds and was now recovering in the comfort of his family's farmhouse. He also relayed her message—that she was too tired and weak to travel back that night, but she would return home the following day.

Sir Gerald and Lady Evans were overjoyed at the news. They had prayed for their daughter's safe return, and their prayers had been answered. The governess, too, was in tears, overwhelmed with gratitude that the young woman she had cared for as her own had been spared from harm.

Sir Gerald, in his gratitude, presented Ferdinand with a magnificent sword, decorated with precious gems. It was a token of appreciation for his bravery and the noble way he had protected their daughter. Ferdinand, ever humble, accepted the gift with gratitude. Sir Gerald was pleased to learn that Ferdinand was Oswald's brother—the same Oswald who was known for his kindness and generosity in the village. Oswald was also the wealthiest landowner in the area, and it pleased Sir Gerald to know that such a man's brother had been the one to save Rosemary.

The Evans family insisted that Ferdinand stay the night, offering him a meal and hospitality he could not refuse. As he sat at their table, enjoying the warm food and company, Ferdinand felt a deep sense of peace. Despite the turmoil of the past days, it was clear that Rosemary's family was grateful and kind, and he felt fortunate to be in their company.

Over the course of the evening, Sir Gerald made plans to host a grand banquet in honor of his daughter's return. Ferdinand, of course, would be the guest of honor, celebrated for his chivalrous actions and the role he had played in saving their beloved Rosemary. Ferdinand, however, was lost in his own thoughts, his heart heavy with the knowledge of Rosemary's secret mission.

He had promised to protect her, but he knew that her journey to the Island of Peace was fraught with danger. The mystery surrounding her mission had troubled him ever since he had learned of it. It seemed like an impossible task, one that would lead her into the unknown. Yet, despite his concerns, Ferdinand was resolute. He would stand by her side through it all, offering his protection and support. No matter how strange or dangerous her mission might seem, he was determined to see it through.

As the evening wore on and Ferdinand was offered a place to rest, he couldn't shake the feeling that this was just the beginning of a much larger adventure—one that would test both his courage and his love for Rosemary. But no matter what challenges lay ahead, he knew he was ready to face them. For Rosemary, he would go anywhere, do anything. He was bound to her, not just by the promise he had made, but by the deep and undeniable bond they shared.

The night in the Sea Castle was one of mixed emotions. While the Evans family rejoiced in their daughter's return, Ferdinand lay awake, troubled by the unknowns of the journey that lay ahead. Rosemary's mission, though shrouded in mystery, had become the center of his thoughts. He had saved her once, but he knew that her path would not be an easy one. Yet, whatever challenges awaited, he was determined to face them, for he had come to realize something profound in the short time they had known each other—he loved Rosemary, and he would do anything to ensure her safety and happiness.

Chapter 11: The Enchanting Melody

Rosemary stood in the heart of the magnificent garden, a place that seemed almost otherworldly in its beauty. It was a garden like no other, bursting with exotic flowers of every color and shape imaginable. The air was fragrant with the scent of blossoms, and the flowers themselves seemed to glow with the first light of dawn. Dew drops glistened on the petals as the sun climbed higher in the sky, casting a golden hue across the landscape. The twittering of birds filled the air, their songs adding to the enchantment of the place. It was a scene of serenity and harmony, where time itself seemed to slow down.

As Rosemary walked through the garden, her mind wandered, taking in the beauty of the moment. "This must be one of the most beautiful places on earth," she thought, her heart swelling with awe. The garden was alive with color and sound, every corner more magical than the last. But despite the beauty surrounding her, her thoughts were fixed on one thing: Ferdinand. She had been waiting anxiously for him, hoping that he would arrive soon to continue the journey they had started together.

As she walked, her attention was drawn to the songs of the larks in the distance. Their sweet melodies seemed to lift her spirit, and before she knew it, she was humming along with them. Her voice, soft and melodic, soon joined the chorus of birdsong, filling the air with its enchanting sound. She found herself sitting by a tranquil pond at the center of the garden, surrounded by swans gliding gracefully on the water. The pond was framed by lush flowering plants, their colors as vibrant as the morning sky. Rosemary, lost in the beauty of the moment, began to sing.

"Let me see thy eyes,
While I am alive,
Let me retrospect,
Before my memories die.
Let me hold thy arm,
And walk around with charm…"

Her voice flowed effortlessly, as if the song had been written just for this moment. The birds, too, seemed to pause and listen, captivated by the young woman's melodic voice. The garden, alive with nature's sounds, now echoed with the haunting beauty of Rosemary's song. She sang all day, her heart full of longing as she waited for Ferdinand's arrival. But as the sun began to set, casting long shadows over the garden, she grew troubled. The evening sky deepened into a rich shade of orange, and still, there was no sign of him.

As darkness fell and the stars began to twinkle above, Rosemary retired to her room, but sleep would not come. She tossed and turned, her thoughts consumed with the mystery of Ferdinand's absence. Unable to rest, she rose from her bed and made her way to the window, gazing out at the moonlit sky. She let her thoughts wander again, and before she knew it, she began to sing once more.

"Let me see thy face,
Before I am awake,
Let me live my dream,
The moonlit sky does wait.
Oh, let me hold thy arm,
Before I quit my dream…"

Her voice, soft and haunting, seemed to carry through the still night air, mingling with the whispers of the wind. But as she sang, a strange feeling overtook her—a sense of confusion, as if the words themselves were not her own. She stopped, suddenly aware that she was no longer in control of the song. It felt as though the verses were coming from another world, speaking of things she couldn't yet understand. With a start, Rosemary sprang from her bed, the dreamlike state shattering around her. It was then that she realized it had all been a dream—a vision, perhaps, but not real.

As dawn began to break, the first rays of light creeping into her room, Rosemary found herself wide awake. She felt no desire to sleep further, her mind still filled with the strange song and the images of Ferdinand she had seen in her dream. When she stepped out of her room, she was surprised to find that the household was already busy, everyone up and about as though nothing had changed. It was a normal morning, yet for Rosemary, everything felt different. The dream still lingered in her mind, as if it had somehow bridged the gap between reality and fantasy, and she could not shake the feeling that something important was about to unfold.

Chapter 12: A Joyful Reunion

Lady Oswald was the first to greet Rosemary that morning, offering her help to prepare for the day ahead. She handed Rosemary a beautiful dress, one that she had kept for special occasions. The gown was a masterpiece, adorned with intricate floral designs that made it appear as though the very essence of the garden had been woven into the fabric. Rosemary slipped into the dress, and when she gazed at her reflection, she marveled at how beautiful it made her feel. The dress fit her perfectly, accentuating her natural grace and beauty. It was a garment fit for a princess, and she couldn't help but feel like one in it.

As Rosemary made her way outside, she saw Ferdinand riding towards the farmhouse. He looked every bit the nobleman, perched atop his horse with the elegance of royalty. His presence was commanding, and yet, there was a warmth about him that made him even more irresistible. Behind him, the Evans family followed in a splendid coach, accompanied by their men. The procession was one of great significance, and it was clear that Sir Gerald and Lady Evans had come to show their gratitude for the hospitality and protection they had received from Oswald and his family.

When the coach arrived at the farmhouse, Oswald and his wife received Sir Gerald and Lady Evans with the utmost respect, welcoming them with open arms. The children, too, presented beautiful bouquets of flowers to their guests, and the Evans family received them with smiles and affection. The reunion was heartfelt, and the emotions ran high as Rosemary embraced her father and stepmother. There were tears of joy and relief, and for the first time in what felt like forever, Rosemary felt the warmth of her family's love surrounding her.

Her stepmother, Lady Evans, held Rosemary close, her embrace full of love and tenderness. It was a moment of deep connection, one that Rosemary had longed for. She had always known that Lady Evans loved her, but now, more than ever, she could feel it in every touch, every word. The bond between them was undeniable, and Rosemary was grateful for the love and care she had received.

Sir Gerald, moved by the kindness of Oswald and his wife, expressed his deep gratitude. He thanked them for protecting his daughter and invited them to join the family for a grand banquet in the evening. It would be a celebration not only of Rosemary's safe return but also of the kindness and generosity that had been shown by Ferdinand and his family. Sir Gerald insisted that Ferdinand be honored for his courage, and he was pleased when Oswald and his family accepted the invitation.

The reunion was full of joy and laughter, and as the day wore on, Sir Gerald and his party prepared to depart for the Sea Castle. Oswald and his wife, having made their plans for the banquet, watched as the coach disappeared into the distance. The children waved goodbye, their hearts full of hope for the future. Ferdinand, too, stood silently, his gaze fixed on the coach as it faded from view. It was a moment of reflection for him, and though he stood there with his family, his thoughts were consumed with what lay ahead. The journey they had started was far from over, and the road ahead promised to be filled with both challenges and triumphs. But for now, he could take solace in the fact that Rosemary was safe, and that she was surrounded by those who loved her.

As the sun set over the horizon, the day's events felt like a dream—one that Rosemary would carry with her always. It was a new beginning, and whatever the future held, she knew she had found a place where she truly belonged.

Chapter 13: A Friend's Warning

In her sunlit gallery, Rosemary delicately worked on a painting, capturing every detail of Ferdinand's likeness. Her brush glided over the canvas, bringing his features to life as if he were standing right before her. The painting was nearly complete when a familiar face appeared—Lenore Winkle, her closest friend, had arrived unannounced. Rosemary's heart lifted at the sight, and the two embraced, their friendship rekindled after weeks apart.

However, Lenore seemed distant, her usually bright demeanor dimmed by an air of worry. Rosemary sensed the change immediately, her happiness mingling with concern. Finally, Lenore spoke, her voice tinged with unease.

"Rosemary," Lenore began, her tone serious. "There is something I need to tell you. I've heard troubling things about my father's dealings with the Witch of the Dark Woods. He's been discussing something valuable—a pearl box, one that belongs to you. He believes it could be dangerous in the wrong hands and wants to take it from you before the witch tries anything drastic. Apparently, she cannot access the Island of Peace without it. Worse still, he fears she might harm you in her quest to obtain it."

Lenore paused, gathering her thoughts. "And there's more. There's talk of a man—a 'chosen one'—who shields you from her. In his presence, her power is weakened, and she can't touch you. For your safety, I beg you to let go of the pearl box."

A soft, incredulous laugh escaped Rosemary. She reassured Lenore, explaining the significance of the "chosen one" and, with a flourish, unveiled her nearly finished painting. "This is him, Lenore," she said, showing her the portrait of Ferdinand. "He is the one."

Relief and joy swept over Lenore's face as she looked at Ferdinand's painted likeness. She congratulated Rosemary, her happiness genuine, and promised to keep her friend in her thoughts and prayers. They spent the rest of the afternoon talking and reminiscing, grateful for this chance to reconnect after Lenore's father, Sir Grey Winkle, had inexplicably kept them apart.

Chapter 14: A Celebration at Sea Castle

The Sea Castle had come alive with the chatter of noble guests. The grand banquet hall gleamed under the light of hundreds of candles, illuminating faces eager to meet Ferdinand, the young man who had risked everything to protect Rosemary. Among the guests, Sir Grey Winkle seemed the most on edge, his gaze constantly shifting as if waiting for something or someone.

Rosemary made a graceful entrance, her gown shimmering in the light, making her appear almost ethereal. Her stepmother, Lady Evans, guided her into the room. As they moved through the crowd, heads turned, and eyes followed Rosemary, captivated by her beauty and elegance.

Then, the doors opened to reveal Ferdinand and his family. Ferdinand was dressed impeccably, and his natural charm and poise made him appear every bit the hero he was. Sir Gerald Evans, Rosemary's father, greeted them warmly, his gratitude evident in the way he spoke to Ferdinand and his family. Sir Grey Winkle, along with many others, looked on in admiration.

The evening was filled with laughter, music, and shared stories. Rosemary introduced Ferdinand to her circle of friends, and particularly to Lenore, whose face lit up at finally meeting the man who meant so much to her friend. She watched with quiet satisfaction as Rosemary presented Ferdinand to others, an unspoken happiness glimmering in her eyes.

Eventually, Rosemary led Ferdinand to her gallery, eager to show him the painting she had created of him. Standing before the portrait, Ferdinand was taken aback.

"You've captured me so well," he said, marveling at her talent. "It's as if you've painted not just my face, but my spirit."

Rosemary's joy was tempered only by the seriousness of what Lenore had confided earlier. She recounted her friend's warning and the rumors of the witch's malevolent intentions. Together, they walked out into the garden, where the beauty of the night seemed at odds with the uncertainty hanging over them.

As they discussed the mysterious pearl box and pondered what they should do, an unexpected disturbance filled the air. Thunder rumbled, and lightning streaked across the sky, casting eerie shadows over the garden. Then, a soft, melodic voice echoed through the air, seeming to come from nowhere and everywhere at once.

"Rosemary, the chosen one," the voice called. "Tell your father that you must embark on a journey with your governess Laura and Ferdinand as your protector. Go to the beach; there, a boat will be waiting for you at a secluded cove. Trust the ocean currents—they will guide you safely to the Island of Peace. Ferdinand must remain by your side until your journey is complete, for he is destined to be more than your protector he is to be your husband. May fortune smile upon you."

The voice faded, leaving Rosemary and Ferdinand standing in stunned silence. The significance of the message was clear, and yet the mystery surrounding their mission only seemed to deepen. After a moment, they exchanged a glance, silently agreeing that they must act quickly.

They hurried back to the castle, where Rosemary sought out her father.

Chapter 15: Journey into the Unknown

Rosemary approached her father, Sir Gerald Evans, with a request that weighed heavily on her heart. She sought permission to embark on a journey, a mission for the welfare of the people on a nearby island who desperately awaited her. Her father listened carefully, his expression a mixture of pride and worry. He hesitated, reluctant to let her go, but when Rosemary mentioned that Ferdinand would be by her side, he softened and granted her permission, albeit reluctantly.

Sir Gerald, along with Lady Evans and the Oswalds, accompanied Rosemary, Ferdinand, and her governess Laura to the secluded creek where a small boat awaited them. The air was filled with a sense of solemnity as they watched the group set off. Sir Gerald and Lady Evans lingered on the shore, their eyes following the boat as it drifted out to sea until it was just a speck on the horizon.

Unbeknownst to them, Sir Grey Winkle had his own plans. Watching from the shadows, he quickly made his way to another boat, hurrying to his hidden yacht with a sinister intent. The witch of the Dark Woods had promised him a substantial reward if he could bring her the mysterious pearl box that Rosemary possessed. To achieve this, he planned to deceive Rosemary into believing the box was cursed and dangerous. His men steered the yacht toward the group's boat, but nature had other plans. A sudden, violent storm arose, thrusting the yacht back toward the port. Frustrated and defeated, Sir Grey abandoned his chase and made his way through the woods, heading toward the witch's lair to confess his failure. Little did he know, the witch had been watching his every move through her enchanted globe.

Meanwhile, Rosemary and her companions sailed undisturbed, unaware of the storm that had thwarted Sir Grey's pursuit. The sea was calm around them, guiding them peacefully as if by some unseen hand. In less than an hour, they reached the island's shore. Climbing out of the boat, they found themselves surrounded by rocks and towering trees, with no immediate signs of human life. Determined to find some sign of civilization, they ventured deeper into the island's dense forest.

Their peaceful exploration was soon interrupted by the roar of distant beasts, a sound that echoed through the trees and sent a chill through Rosemary. She looked around, frightened, and her first instinct was to return to the boat. But when they arrived back at the creek, the boat was gone, leaving them stranded. Fear crept into their hearts as they wondered if this was a trap laid by someone with dark intentions.

Ferdinand, however, remained undeterred. He unsheathed his sword, his stance poised and ready for any threat that might come their way. Rosemary clutched the pearl box tightly, her knuckles pale as she prayed silently for Ferdinand's safety. He moved forward with quiet determination, leading them away from the shore and closer to the sounds of the wild animals. He advanced cautiously, with Rosemary and Laura following close behind, their faces pale with fear but trusting in his protection.

As they pressed on, Ferdinand's senses remained sharp, prepared to defend his companions against any danger. Every step took them deeper into the unknown, yet Ferdinand's bravery inspired Rosemary to stay calm, even as her heart raced with uncertainty.

Chapter 16: Schemes in the Shadows

As the sun dipped below the horizon, casting long shadows over the land, Sir Grey Winkle finally arrived at the witch's cave, hidden deep within the woods. The cave emanated an eerie, unnatural energy, but Sir Grey swallowed his fear and entered, steeling himself to face her wrath.

The witch greeted him with a sneer, her voice dripping with sarcasm. "Welcome, King of the Cowards," she mocked, her eyes glinting with contempt.

Sir Grey opened his mouth to explain the storm that had foiled his plans, but the witch cut him off with a furious roar. "Do you take me for a fool?" she snapped. "I've seen everything. Your pathetic efforts were nothing short of an embarrassment. You let a mere storm stop you, when I commanded you to retrieve the box, even if it meant taking Rosemary's life!"

"But," he stammered, a tremor of fear in his voice, "she is like a daughter to me. I couldn't harm her."

The witch's eyes blazed with fury as she advanced toward him. "Do not speak to me of weakness, you miserable worm!" she spat. "Leave my sight before I turn you to dust!"

Her words sliced through the air like a knife, and Sir Grey staggered backward, his face pale with fear. Defeated and humiliated, he retreated from the cave, his shoulders slumped. As he made his way back to the Sea Castle, regret gnawed at his heart. For the first time, he silently prayed for the safety of Rosemary and Ferdinand, hoping they would remain beyond the reach of the witch's dark powers.

Chapter 17: Enchanted Discoveries

Ferdinand, Rosemary, and Laura cautiously peered through a thick wall of bushes, and the scene that lay before them took their breath away. By a serene pond, lions lounged beside sheep, oxen mingled with horses, and even crocodiles basked peacefully on the banks, observing the tranquil gathering. Animals that were natural enemies seemed to be united here in a harmony beyond imagination.

"Could this be heaven?" Rosemary whispered, her eyes wide with awe.

"This is remarkable," Ferdinand replied, equally spellbound. "I could never have dreamed of such a place."

At that moment, a majestic seahorse—a mystical creature Rosemary had only spoken of in stories—sprinted toward her with joy. She gasped, recognizing the creature from her childhood tales and sharing her excitement with Ferdinand, who was deeply moved by the sight.

But the surprises didn't end there. The seahorse halted before them, reared up, and in a commanding voice, proclaimed, "Let the promises of the Oyster Queen be fulfilled by the power of the Pearl Box."

Suddenly, the pearl box in Rosemary's hands began to tremble. Startled, she instinctively threw it into the air. The box shattered mid-flight, scattering brilliant pearls in all directions. A thunderous sound echoed through the skies, lightning streaked across the heavens, and an intense, radiant light enveloped the island, forcing them to close their eyes.

When they opened their eyes, silence blanketed the island. They found themselves surrounded by a sea of pearls, which lay scattered so densely that the ground was barely visible. And as if conjured by magic, the once-empty island now bustled with people. These islanders were adorned with fine pearl jewelry, and they bowed before Ferdinand and Rosemary with reverence. To the couple's astonishment, each now wore a gleaming pearl crown.

Meanwhile, in a dark cave on the mainland, the witch who had conspired against Rosemary and Ferdinand stared into her enchanted globe, only to watch it shatter in her hands. In a flash, she melted away, as powerless as an icicle in a roaring fire, vanquished by the box's divine magic.

Ferdinand, Rosemary, and Laura were so stunned by this otherworldly transformation that words escaped them. The people of the island, full of gratitude, organized a royal celebration to honor their new leaders. They led the group to a magnificent carriage drawn by pristine white horses, which carried them to the heart of the island and toward a grand palace that seemed to sparkle under the sun's glow.

Once inside the palace, the island's priest approached Ferdinand and Rosemary. He revealed that they were the prophesied rulers who would bring prosperity to the island, fulfilling the promises made by the Oyster Queen. He gently urged them to marry and rule the island as king and queen, a request met with both surprise and wonder.

Three elders then stepped forward to share a story that had been passed down through generations—a tale nearly 300 years old, holding the key to this mysterious island's history. Ferdinand and Rosemary listened intently, captivated by the legend that had guided the fate of this island and its people.

Chapter 18: The Legend of the Peaceful Kingdom

The first elder spoke, his voice echoing through the grand hall. "Three hundred years ago, our island was ruled by a wise and noble king named Goodwill. He was a peaceful leader, a man of strength and compassion, who brought great wealth and harmony to our people. However, he lacked an heir, and our island's riches made it vulnerable to the envy and aggression of outsiders."

The elder's eyes gleamed with pride as he continued, "Despite the dangers, King Goodwill loved exploration. With each voyage, he returned with treasures and knowledge from distant lands. On one such journey, the seas turned eerily calm, yet his ship was suddenly tossed about as if by unseen forces. Strange voices filled the air, crying for salvation amidst wild, echoing roars."

Another elder stepped forward to continue the tale. "It was then that a monstrous octopus emerged from the depths of the ocean. It was hunting oysters in vast numbers, ravaging the very creatures responsible for creating pearls. Among them was the Oyster Queen herself, pleading for help, for the giant octopus threatened to annihilate her kingdom."

"The Queen's cries struck the king's heart, and he resolved to protect the oysters. He and his crew fought valiantly, and after a fierce battle, the king managed to kill the octopus, but not before it delivered a deadly sting. The Oyster Queen emerged from the waves, her face filled with gratitude."

The elder bowed his head, recounting the Queen's words. "'Noble King,' she said, 'you have saved my kingdom from destruction, and for this, I bless your island. Henceforth, no blood shall be shed upon your shores. Lions and other beasts will eat grass and live peacefully among men. The people of your land will be honest, and even the smallest theft shall be unheard of."

The second elder then added, "The Oyster Queen blessed King Goodwill's people with peace and purity. She foretold that the island would be shielded from enemies by ocean currents and storms, and it would remain unruled for three centuries. Then, when the time was right, a seahorse would bring forth a chosen prince and princess, who would bear a pearl box—a sign of the Queen's promise. This box would bring prosperity to the island and unite the chosen rulers who would usher in an era of peace."

The third elder, with a solemn look, took over the story. "Upon his return, the king recounted this tale to his people. He grew ill from the octopus's sting and passed away after months of suffering. Since then, our ancestors have awaited the prophecy's fulfillment, passing down the story of the chosen rulers who would come to bring peace and prosperity."

As the elders concluded the tale, Rosemary and Ferdinand exchanged glances, understanding the depth of their connection to this island and its people. They nodded in agreement to the priest's request, but with one condition—they wished to invite their families to share in their joyous union. The priest and the people, overjoyed, readily agreed, for they, too, were eager to welcome the family of their new rulers.

The islanders rejoiced, thrilled by the fulfillment of the ancient prophecy. With Ferdinand and Rosemary as their king and queen, the Island of Peace was set to enter a new era, one filled with hope, harmony, and boundless prosperity. And so, amidst an island draped in pearls and blessings, the stage was set for a kingdom unlike any other—a land where love, peace, and unity would forever reign.

Chapter 19: A Joyful Reunion and a Royal Wedding

As the first rays of dawn broke over the horizon, a ship prepared to leave the island's harbor for the first time in three centuries. Seven islanders, carrying important scrolls, sailed toward the mainland to deliver messages to Sir Gerald and Oswald. Their journey was guided by fate and purpose, and they were pleased to find the Sea Castle just a short distance from shore, glimmering with the light of morning.

The castle guards, surprised by the visitors, quickly informed Sir Gerald Evans that messengers had arrived with news from his beloved daughter, Rosemary. Sir Gerald welcomed the visitors warmly, eager to receive their message. Opening the scroll, he read Rosemary's heartfelt words describing her remarkable journey, the treasures of the island, and her newfound duty as Queen. With joy in her words, Rosemary requested her father's blessing for her marriage to Ferdinand and her role as Queen of the island.

With the message delivered, the Evans family and the messengers set off together toward Oswald's farmhouse in two splendid carriages. When Oswald and his wife saw the Evans family arriving, their faces lit up, though a hint of disappointment flickered as they realized Ferdinand was not with them. Their joy returned, however, as they read the scroll, learning of Ferdinand's adventures and his fate on the island. The messengers assured them that a ship awaited them all, ready to carry them to the island for the wedding and coronation.

Without delay, Sir Gerald and Oswald decided to journey to the island that very evening, accompanied by their families. The two groups boarded boats that carried them safely to the ship. By nightfall, the ship set sail, embarking on a journey to the island to fulfill Rosemary and Ferdinand's dreams.

The next morning, as the ship neared the harbor, Ferdinand, Rosemary, and the people of the island gathered to welcome the first visitors they had seen in over three hundred years. The islanders prepared two magnificent coaches, adorned with garlands and symbols of peace, to escort the guests to the palace. Sir Gerald and Lady Evans were awestruck as they took in the magical beauty of the Seahorse, which astonished them by speaking, expressing gratitude for their kindness.

Once settled, the priest approached the Evans family and the other guests to discuss the timing of the wedding. It was decided that Ferdinand and Rosemary would marry the next day. The guests were then shown to their luxurious chambers, each room prepared with elegance, honoring the reunion and the beginning of a new era for the island.

Throughout the day, the islanders prepared for the royal wedding, making every arrangement a symbol of the fulfillment of the Oyster Queen's promise. The people rejoiced, sensing that a bright new chapter was unfolding on their island—a chapter of love, peace, and prosperity.

Chapter 20: A Wedding to Unite Two Worlds

The following morning, the island was buzzing with anticipation. The entire community gathered outside the island's ancient church, eager to witness the royal wedding. The choir of children sang a joyful melody, filling the air with a sense of unity and hope as the bridal coach approached.

When Rosemary stepped out, the crowd gasped in awe. She was radiant, a vision in her wedding attire, her veil cascading behind her like a mist of morning light. Children, full of cheer and wonder, carried the long train of her veil, adding to the magical atmosphere. Through the delicate tulle, her face shone with the warmth and glow of happiness, like the moon glimpsed through a soft, translucent cloud.

Sir Gerald proudly escorted his daughter down the aisle. Soft music played as they walked, and bells chimed gently overhead, marking each step toward a new beginning. The guests watched in admiration, captivated by the serene beauty of the moment.

At the altar stood Ferdinand, waiting for his bride. His tall and chivalrous presence radiated strength and nobility, and he seemed to embody the spirit of a valiant knight, calm yet resolute. As Rosemary joined him, the crowd looked on in wonder at the ideal couple they made, each a perfect reflection of the other's grace and courage.

The island priest officiated the ceremony, bestowing upon Ferdinand and Rosemary not only the bond of marriage but the title of King and Queen. It was a union not just of two people, but of two worlds, each bringing hope and light to the other.

After the wedding, a grand banquet awaited the guests in the palace's majestic hall, which had been beautifully adorned for the occasion. Portraits of King Goodwill and his predecessors lined the walls, each a reminder of the island's noble history. Sir Gerald marveled at the grandeur of the hall, proud that his daughter's portrait would soon join those of the island's great rulers, marking the beginning of a new legacy.

As everyone settled in for the banquet, the priest once again recounted the legend of the Island of Peace, sharing the inspiring story with the guests who were new to its magic. The tale of King Goodwill's bravery and the blessings bestowed by the Oyster Queen filled the room with awe. Sir Gerald, listening to the story of a land where peace reigned and conflict was unknown, felt immense pride and joy that his daughter was now part of such a unique and noble kingdom.

Raising his glass, Sir Gerald offered his blessing to the newlyweds, wishing them a long life filled with peace and prosperity. And in that moment, as the islanders celebrated the union of their new King and Queen, it was clear that the promises of the Oyster Queen had indeed come to fruition. The Island of Peace had regained its former glory, and its future looked brighter than ever.

Chapter 21 A Royal Ascension

After three centuries of silence, the grand hall of the palace brimmed with excitement and anticipation. The islanders, who had waited patiently for the fulfillment of the Oyster Queen's ancient promises, now gathered to witness the crowning of their new King and Queen. Ferdinand and Rosemary, the chosen couple whose actions had brought prosperity back to the island, would soon ascend the thrones of the Island of Peace.

Clad in elegant robes, Ferdinand and Rosemary walked down the central aisle, hand in hand. Their calm and dignified demeanor inspired admiration from the onlookers as they approached the thrones, symbols of a legacy that had lain dormant for generations. With a solemn smile, the priest welcomed them, his voice steady as he led the couple through the traditional vows. With gentle hands, he placed the royal crowns upon their heads, formally declaring them King Ferdinand and Queen Rosemary. In Ferdinand's hand, he placed a staff that shimmered with a celestial glow, a symbol of his newfound authority and the unbroken promise of peace.

"Long live King Ferdinand!" proclaimed the priest, his voice echoing through the hall. The people responded in unison, their voices rising with reverence.

"And long live Queen Rosemary!" the priest continued, and once again, the crowd joined, their voices a chorus of loyalty and hope.

Ferdinand and Rosemary exchanged glances, humbled by the momentousness of the occasion. Their journey to this day had been filled with challenges and trials, yet here they stood, the fulfillment of the island's ancient prophecy. The lavish ceremony and the overwhelming devotion of the people felt surreal, as though they were caught in a beautiful dream.

In recognition of the island's abundance, the palace treasury overflowed with lustrous pearls—a testament to the prosperity that had returned to the island. The islanders, too, possessed pearls beyond their means to store, a gift from the sea's depths that marked the restoration of harmony.

As his first act as King, Ferdinand extended a hand to the world beyond the island's shores. He formally requested that Sir Gerald and Oswald serve as ambassadors, carrying an invitation to Her Majesty, the Queen of England, to visit the newly reborn island. The invitation, a scroll bearing Ferdinand's seal, was a bridge between the island and the wider world. He presented Sir Gerald and Oswald with three ornate boxes filled with exquisite pearl jewelry, gifts from the island's people, to offer to Her Majesty as a symbol of goodwill.

In addition to the gifts for the Queen, Ferdinand extended his gratitude to the families who had supported him and Rosemary. He presented three boxes of pearl treasures to the Evans and three to the Oswalds. The families accepted these tokens with warmth, grateful for the honor and deeply moved by the island's gesture.

Chapter 22: The Farewell Voyage

With the coronation complete and the island's future secured, it was time for the magical Seahorse to return to the sea. Its mission fulfilled, the Seahorse prepared to bid farewell to its new King and Queen. As it approached the shore, it bowed its majestic head, blessing Ferdinand and Rosemary one last time. Tears welled up in Rosemary's eyes as she watched the magnificent creature slowly wade into the waters, its shimmering form a vision of strength and grace.

The gathered crowd gasped as the Seahorse began to transform, its majestic shape gradually shrinking until it became a small, delicate seahorse once more. In its final form, the Seahorse swam into the depths of the sea, disappearing into the horizon. Sir Gerald and Lady Evans, standing nearby, marveled at the transformation, enchanted by the mystical farewell. They could not help but think how lucky their daughter was to have shared such a magical bond with a creature of legend.

Before departing, Rosemary made a heartfelt request to her governess to remain on the island with her. The governess, touched by Rosemary's plea, gladly consented, choosing to stay by her side in this new chapter of her life.

Finally, the day arrived for the Evans, the Oswalds, and the other guests to leave the island. They boarded the ship that would carry them back to England, leaving with fond memories and a profound respect for the island and its people. The islanders, showing the same kindness that had welcomed their guests, provided boats to transport them safely to the ship. Laden with the gift boxes filled with pearl ornaments, the islanders ensured that every box reached the Sea Castle without incident before bidding farewell to the departing guests.

Lady Oswald, accompanied by her children, Edward and Annie, took a splendid carriage arranged by Sir Gerald for their journey back to the Sea Castle. Their hearts filled with gratitude, they carried with them not only the memories of the island but also the beautiful gifts of pearl jewelry, given to them as a symbol of the island's appreciation.

Upon arriving at the castle, Lady Evans carefully examined the three boxes of pearl treasures, marveling at the intricate beauty of each piece. As she wore the pearls, she felt a deep sense of joy and pride, cherishing these gifts as reminders of the magical land that her daughter now ruled.

With little time to waste, Sir Gerald and Oswald prepared to deliver the island's invitation to the Queen of England. Together, they set off, determined to share the wonder of the Island of Peace with the world beyond its shores.

Chapter 23: A Royal Encounter

Upon arrival in England, Sir Gerald and Oswald were granted an audience with Her Royal Highness, the Queen. As they entered the grand hall, they presented the three intricately decorated boxes filled with dazzling pearl jewelry—a gift from King Ferdinand and Queen Rosemary of the Island of Peace. The gentlemen recounted the story of the island, a place where humans and wild creatures lived in harmony, untouched by violence or bloodshed, and where the people had come to cherish peace as their most sacred value.

The Queen listened intently, her expression shifting from curiosity to genuine admiration as she learned of the island's unique ways. The notion of a land where no blood was shed, and where even wild beasts coexisted peacefully with humans, captivated her imagination. She found herself moved by the account of King Ferdinand and Queen Rosemary, leaders of such a remarkable realm. With a deep sense of respect, the Queen accepted the invitation to visit this extraordinary island, as well as the magnificent pearls, which she recognized as symbols of the island's bountiful peace and prosperity.

In turn, Her Majesty expressed her gratitude with lavish gifts of her own: gold, rare gemstones, and precious artifacts, each item carefully selected as a tribute to the King and Queen of the Island of Peace. Overwhelmed by her kindness and generosity, Sir Gerald and Oswald conveyed their heartfelt thanks and departed with high hopes, eager to share the Queen's response with their beloved King and Queen.

Returning to the island, the ambassadors joyfully relayed the Queen's acceptance of the invitation and presented her gifts. King Ferdinand and Queen Rosemary were deeply touched by the Queen's goodwill and support. The warmth and sincerity of the exchange symbolized a promising alliance between the Island of Peace and England.

Chapter 24: The Queen's Visit and the Peace Treaty

Her Royal Highness, the Queen of England, eventually made her long-awaited journey to the Island of Peace. As her ship approached the shores, the sight that greeted her was enchanting—a vibrant landscape bathed in sunlight, where lush greenery met the sea and wild creatures roamed freely among the people. Ferdinand and Rosemary welcomed her with open arms, their joy evident as they guided her through the island's harmonious world.

The Queen was captivated by the island's tranquility and was struck by the sight of animals wandering without fear among the people. There were no fences or chains, no sense of hierarchy among species, just a collective peace that pervaded every corner of the land. Touched by what she witnessed, the Queen felt inspired to secure this exceptional place against any threats that might disrupt its serenity. Thus, she pledged her kingdom's protection and signed a peace treaty, assuring that England would stand by the island's side in times of need.

In addition to the peace treaty, the Queen and King Ferdinand agreed upon a trade alliance. This partnership promised an exchange of pearls for precious goods, which would further enrich both England and the Island of Peace. As the Queen signed these agreements, she made a declaration that would forever honor the island's reputation, pronouncing it "the most peaceful place on Earth." Her admiration for the island was so profound that she promised to return frequently, eager to experience its unmatched tranquility whenever possible.

This new alliance led to an era of abundance for the islanders. They traded pearls for rare goods from afar, adding to their prosperity. Their land was blessed with fragrant, colorful flowers blooming everywhere, filling the air with a gentle, sweet scent. The fields yielded abundant crops, and lush pastures stretched across the island, providing plentiful grazing for the animals. Since none of the animals were predators, they roamed together peacefully, thriving in an ecosystem defined by balance and mutual respect.

Chapter 25: A Realm of Lasting Harmony

As the days passed, the island flourished beyond what anyone could have imagined. The ocean currents and strong winds acted as natural guardians, warding off pirates and unwanted visitors. Only those with good intentions were able to reach its shores, drawn to its reputation as a place of tranquility and prosperity. Countries from distant lands soon sought peaceful relations with the Island of Peace, leading to additional treaties that strengthened its position as a respected and prosperous land. These agreements strictly forbade any trading or sale of animals, protecting the beloved wildlife that had become a cherished part of the island's identity.

With each passing season, the island's beauty continued to grow. The people, content and secure, enjoyed the fruits of their labor and the richness of their land. The cheerful songs of the island's birds became a constant melody, filling every moment with a joyful harmony that seemed to reflect the very soul of the island itself.

The Evans and the Oswalds frequently returned to visit Ferdinand and Rosemary, who welcomed them with open hearts. Oswald, who had risen in political stature in England, was no longer merely a wealthy landowner but a respected figure with influence. Their bond with the King and Queen remained strong, a testament to the enduring friendships that had blossomed on the island.

Rosemary's governess, Laura, chose to remain on the island at Rosemary's request, serving as her legal advisor and loyal companion. Her wisdom proved invaluable in helping Rosemary navigate her new role as Queen. Yet, when Sir Gerald's family expanded with the birth of his son, Richmond Evans, Laura returned to England after a year, ready to support the family once again.

Under the wise and compassionate rule of King Ferdinand and Queen Rosemary, the Island of Peace continued to prosper, setting an example for other nations. Its reputation as a realm of peace and abundance only grew, attracting admiration from far and wide. For as long as they reigned, Ferdinand and Rosemary cherished the island and its people, governing with kindness and integrity. Together, they lived in harmony with their subjects, their love for each other and their kingdom cementing a legacy of peace that would be remembered for generations to come.

THE END

The edits and layout of this print version are Copyright © 2024
By Jessica Hintz